HALF DEAD

I COULDN'T BREATHE.

AARCHI ADVANI SAINI

ISBN 979-888546136-8

I couldn't breathe, life itself felt as though it became heavier. Friendships became harder to maintain and my smile faded away with each passing day. I was alone, I was broken, and I was desperate. My entire life became the opposite of what I was aiming for. I faced the world with screaming eyes and a broken heart and yet I wore a mask that showed happiness and joy. My days usually went the same: attend class, sleep in and talk to people who didn't really matter to me, Or the only one who matters. I aimed for love, I aimed for acknowledgment. I aimed for a new beginning.

Contents

Preface

I couldn't breathe, life itself felt as though it became heavier. Friendships became harder to maintain and my smile faded away with each passing day. I was alone, I was broken, and I was desperate. My entire life became the opposite of what I was aiming for. I faced the world with screaming eyes and a broken heart and yet I wore a mask that showed happiness and joy. My days usually went the same: attend class, sleep in and talk to people who didn't really matter to me, Or the only one who matters. I aimed for love, I aimed for acknowledgment. I aimed for a new beginning.

Author

Aarchi Advani Saini.!

[ ] Author of the book "The Loads Of Poetry"

[ ] Social media "Aarchi Advani Saini"

[ ] Aries, believe in destiny.

[ ] Author of the book "The Loads Of Poetry Part One and Two", "The Journey of Love", "The Way to Love", "The Anonymous", "Let's be Confidante", "The Cabalistic Child ", "Confession", "Dark Dead", "Faith is All", "The Street of Paris", and more.

Aarchi Advani Saini.!

She becomes one of the youngest author of her hometown Shamli. For this Danik Jagran newspaper covers this news, Later, many news channels interviewed her. So renowned for "The loads of poetry). She has sold the book worldwide, the recipient of numerous prestigious awards in her writing journey. She writes daily columns syndicated throughout the world. Aarchi Advani is well known for her writing on many other platforms. She is also a fantasy and literary fiction author specializing in "Life", as well as her upcoming book "Lifeless Life."

She publish her 10th book as her Hindi novel called "papa". She also hosts a channel where she uses her passion for storytelling. And a background in business to help other creatives navigate their writing. So she is compiling an anthology named, "Of Your Choice", And her publishing journey is another level, she is good at her writing skills, but no one knows how to write books, same with her, but with the passage of time, she grows. When she's not writing or tubing she enjoys listening to books,

Making stories on her own. And love to live in her virtual world.

CHAPTER ONE

"Lies"

Lifeless skies filled my vision. I watched as the break of dawn filled it with life, removing the emptiness it once felt. Understanding that everything in life had a purpose but most importantly, supported each other. I was young, yet my heart craved for warmth and sincerity. I knew how fragile I was, and yet I hid it away from everyone else. Running from person to person hoping to find what I was looking for, only to be disappointed in the end. I knew I was a terrible person for doing this; creating a home filled with empty promises, only to tear it down with the truth. Friends never stayed; knowing I had done wrong to those who didn't deserve it but also giving my loyalty to those who didn't appreciate it. I felt trapped in loneliness, as though the walls were slowly closing in on me. Hiding it from my own blood, my smile seemed sincere yet nobody looked into my eyes. It was like living in a prison cell, waiting for someone to free me but also wondering if the keys were lost.

Sighing, I looked at the serious man next to me. Showing no interest in making conversation, I should be used to this. One would think we had no bond, no ties, and yet I could never walk away from my own blood. Closing my eyes, the road felt long. Every day my Dad took me to class, it was quite the distance. I had no other transport option because he refused to accept the fact that I'm finally growing up. I was no longer in high school, that little girl had to grow up and yet everyone kept pulling me down. Deep in thought, I didn't realize we had arrived at campus.

"What time?" said a deep and uninterested voice.

"I really don't know, I'll call you." Lies. I knew my schedule off by heart, but all I needed was an escape from reality. A reality where I could be someone totally different, someone happy. "Bye" I said, matching his tone of voice. Once he acknowledged my greeting, I closed the door. I felt the wind dance on my skin as I entered the campus door. I wore my mask with pride, I gave a deep smile to each person that walked by. Eventually I saw the closest person to me, someone who I was certain could be real, Amy. Running towards her, I squished her in a hug. She giggled. She was a bright character that never stopped smiling, she was someone who I wanted to imitate.

"So how's Spots?" She asked interest evident in her eyes. I laughed, and shook my head. Amy and I usually came up with nicknames for guys we "liked". However, I wasn't sure if I actually liked this guy. To be honest, I wasn't sure if I liked anyone, but I forced myself to believe otherwise. I was so obsessed with trying to find where I belonged that I searched for a place in others who sparked my interest. Failing with every try, I ended up speaking to Spots. However, I was stuck in something that I no longer wanted. As much as I tried to break free, I couldn't bring myself to break John's heart. Terrible of me, I know. He grew attached while I grew distant, a relationship without the actual title. I was trapped. I didn't want to break his heart, but I knew I had to in order for mine to move on.

"I actually saw him at the event, it wasn't planned. I mean, I didn't feel like going but he was actually really cute. We threw small sticks at each other, it was so weird." Smiling, I appreciated his friendship. When my Dad ran off for about a week with no trace whatsoever he remained positive, not knowing

the full story. However, the positivity spoke volumes while my knowledge gave in.

"Oh wow Melissa, you seem really happy." As soon as the conversation started, it came to an end. Everyone began moving to class, fearing they'd be late while others had no care in the world. Slowly making my way towards class, I happily greeted the few classmates that allowed me to laugh and have fun with them.

"Suuup" said a very energetic Josh. I smiled warmly before greeting back. He was a weird character, but in a good way. He never seemed to be in a bad mood and always had this positivity about him that pulled me towards him.

"Wazzzzup... I'm just feeling tired." I replied and Josh looked at me surprisingly.

"You just got here." I raised my eyebrow at his response.

"So? It's me you're talking to here. You know how I am." Not even phased, he just shook his head before putting in his earphones. As I made my way towards my seat, our teacher came rushing past me. It was only then that I realized, this was going to be an extremely long day.

CHAPTER TWO

"Mistakes"

As class finally came to an end, I had to rush home. This was no ordinary day where I could avoid being at home. No, it was my cousin's high-school farewell. As much as it pained me to go, I wanted to create a bond with my cousins. Pretty farfetched considering they don't like me. Personality-wise, we all clashed. Everyone viewed me as the little girl who does nothing wrong, the girl who lived on her high horse, and the girl who was so spoilt that she just couldn't relate to anyone. In actual fact, I had done everything wrong. I made mistakes that broke me. I was the one who needed friends not judgment. I was the one who wasn't spoiled because her family struggled financially. I guess I could understand where they were coming from though because I never saw them nor did I show I was hurting. I wanted a fresh start but nobody was willing to start with me.

Throwing on my old high school club shirt, I refused to put in any effort. I expected this visit to be as short as possible. Looking in the mirror, I asked myself "Ready to turn invisible?" My Mom walked in, excitement filled the atmosphere. Possibly because she was going to see her family. That rarely happens these days and when it does, war breaks out in our household. Seeing her family become a mission with increasing difficulty and watching all her sisters grow together became even harder because my mom couldn't experience that growth with them. My Dad held a personal grudge against her family and nobody could understand why. We were fully aware that whenever went to the family, we'd return to arguments. It was a never-ending battle, leaving scars that wouldn't heal. Fake smiling with everyone because time was precious, I pretended for my Mom's sake. I accepted being ignored if it meant she could be happy for a few hours.

Once we reached my aunt's house, I took a look inside. Turquoise and white beautifully covered the house, the sisters really amaze everyone when it comes to working together for a family cause. My eyes fell on my cousin. She was older than I was but she always welcomed me in when all my other female cousins my age refused to acknowledge me. Walking towards her, I smiled.

"Hi, Shannon." She turned and smiled my way.

"Hey, Melissa." Before we could continue speaking, we were asked to help set the table. Being me, I didn't know where to put anything. Taking the drinks, I tried placing them on the table, only to feel them wobble from the weight. Decorating was seriously not my forte. Placing it on the table I walked to the door. Before I knew it, I was face to face with a female cousin who was only a year older than me, Lilith. Surprisingly enough she acknowledged me. I never understood what I had done to her but for years, she and my younger cousin made me out to be the outsider. Maybe it was because we had different interests or maybe I just wasn't cool enough. Either way, they never gave me room in their little circle, always leaving me out in the cold. Noticing she came with her new boyfriend, he didn't greet me at all. Actually, he refused to look my way. Sighing, I wondered what was said about me this time around.

I thought it best to brush it off and I went back to Shannon. I saw her smile fade and I could see the visible look of disapproval dancing on her face as Lilith sat with her new boyfriend. But who could blame her, she had a personal family issue with Lilith who didn't seem to care about her opinion in the slightest. I ignored it and our attention was quickly drawn to Shannon's brother, Vincent. Vincent has been away from home for about a few months now, he's been focusing on his goals at the Police Training Camp and his dedication to his goal was evident in his appearance. Shannon enveloped Vincent in a hug, asking why he never told her that he was coming. You could hear the excitement in her voice to be reunited with her brother. It was a sweet sibling reunion as I watched them smile through their eyes. Soon, I hugged Vincent, welcoming him back, even if it was just for short while.

I watched the siblings enjoy each other's light-hearted company as they caught up on each other's lives. Laughing with them, I felt a part of something instead of being all alone. Shannon eventually started questioning me about Spots, curious as to how things were going. Spots and I had met on a very strange note, technically we didn't speak with words but always with a casual wave. As I was about to leave Vincent's house, Spots pulled up and chatted away with Vincent, while I waited inside for my mother. As I walked out, we politely waved until Vincent's mother shouted that he was staring at me. My mom rushed to the car and told me to get in while he awkwardly fell back in his seat.

"He's been asking for your number, the poor guy." Said an amused Shannon.

"Yeah, we've been chatting and it's been good," I replied honestly, accepting that I appreciated his friendship.

"By the way, about the lift with Zack. What are the arrangements? Because I'm well aware how strict your father can be." Switching the topic to something I was trying to avoid, I inwardly sighed. Apart from me did not want to travel with this lift club. Not that I had a problem with Zack, but it would be awkward trying to make conversation with someone who was basically a stranger. Also considering the fact that I'm really awkward at first, I could just mess up without having to use words. Another problem was that he dated Lilith, the cousin who treated me like dirt. That makes things extremely awkward for me. I appreciated the idea but was I really up for something so new and awkward.

"I don't know, I haven't asked my parents yet actually, but it would be cool," I replied in the nicest way I could think of. I didn't want to come off as rude, they were trying to help me and I realized that, but there were too many 'buts' that I couldn't bring myself to ask.

"I mean, it's basically family so it's not with a complete stranger." Sadly, he was a stranger to me. We've met in the past, but I was too young to remember most of it and he was focused on Lilith that I never really formed a friendship with him. I knew absolutely nothing about him.

"I guess, I'll ask my parents and let you know," I replied, wondering if I'll even ask or if I'll just mention it as an idea that could be brushed off.

Suddenly there was a commotion, I assumed that my cousin had arrived. Taking a peek, my eyes fell on her as she came in. As elegant as ever, she resembled an actual princess. Suddenly, I noticed a girl from my previous school and I smiled. We had a rough past of not liking each other but we outgrew it. Waving at her, my mind wandered to my ex-best friend, Katy. They're still pretty close, but Katy and I aren't. Growing up with her, it hurt to know that we don't speak anymore but what was meant to be always found its way back. Noticing that she was not alone, I saw Amy's brother, also known as the boyfriend.

Quickly greeting, I saw my cousin slip out. This was my chance to make things right or try to. I never really saw her, maybe I could show her I wasn't the person everyone made me out to be. Try to show her that deep down, I was the same. Being more responsible didn't mean I could never relate to anyone, I would always try if it meant creating a bond. Seeing her quickly run out the gate, I called out to her. "You look really pretty Minnie!" She didn't even look at me. Her attention was so focused on everyone else that I just got a side glance and a mumbled thank you. Maybe I'm not cut out for this.

Looking at my phone, I tiredly read my messages. As expected, I received messages from John. I couldn't bring myself to reply, a sense of commitment that I wasn't willing to provide anymore. Instead of doing the proper thing, I typed 'off' on my status. Staring at his chat, I shrugged and went off. Everything about him clung to me, squeezing away at the life I wanted to live.

Returning to Shannon, I overheard them say they're about to leave. They suggested that they could drop me at home but I really wanted to see Shannon's new flat with Vincent and James, my other cousin. Surprisingly, my mom allowed me to drive with them. Shyly letting out the fact that I want to see the new house, they eventually agreed.

We eventually arrived at a pink building after a few stops along the way. The area seemed peaceful actually. Walking inside, I saw the flight of stairs and I sighed. The effort felt too real. Dragging myself up the stairs, I was happy to see that their flat was on the second floor. Not realizing that once their front door opened, my whole world would change.

CHAPTER THREE

"Light-hearted smile"

The door opened with a loud thud as I watched Shannon's twin daughters run around inside without a care in the world. I froze. Looking in front of me, my eyes landed on Zack. I felt tense up, I didn't expect anyone else to be here. Remembering that he lived here, I moped. Why couldn't he have gone out or something? He looked serious as he played video games. Maybe he wouldn't notice me. Shyly greeting him, he acknowledged my presence. Quickly turning away from him, I saw another new face and I inwardly cried. Why didn't anyone warn me?!

After an awkward introduction, I found my way to the couch. Glancing at Zack, I couldn't help but stare. It had been so long since I last saw him; I noted the change in his appearance and how he still caught my eye regardless. He didn't seem interested in making any conversation, not that I minded, my nerves couldn't handle it if he did. Remembering the small crush I had on him, I looked away. That was a very long time ago.

My lips felt dry and plain, uncomfortably reaching for my lip-gloss, I immediately regretted it. James, being the usual jokey person that he is, screeched out:

"Melissa, who are you putting that lip gloss on for? Is it for Zack's friend? I'm watching you!" I felt my face begin to burn. I had just met Randy, Zack's friend.

"I'm not!" I looked down as I said that, making sure to avoid all eye contact.

"Randy has a baby on the way; he cant be catching on shit like that." Said a laughing Shannon. The awkwardness grew. He was going to be a father? Emphasis on father! How did I manage to land myself in such an awkward situation? I was more focused on Zack than Randy. That's just my luck.

It was over in a split second as James and Vincent made their way out the door. Falling on the couch, Zack followed. Leaving a decent amount of space between us, I tensed up. He chose to sit closer to me when there were other seats open. Was I reading the signs correctly or was I being delusional? Hearing a knock on the door, my brother Brian made his way in. Taking a seat between us, I sighed. Always leave it to my brother to read the signs with me.

Before I knew it, James and Vincent had returned but Zack and Randy were nowhere to be found. Maybe they finally decided that this was lame and wanted out. Not long after, I saw Zack pull up with a new person who I assumed to be his friend. His friend, William, looked friendly as he carried a platter of snacks, probably as a housewarming gift.

Deciding to sit on the floor, I sighed. This night seemed to be taking the turn for the worst. Looking up, I noticed Zack come outside. I was surprised. He seemed more anti-social than an actual social butterfly. Seeing him take a glass of alcohol, I blinked. He drinks? I never imagined him to drink, especially out of Barbie's plastic cup.

Eventually, he sat down in front of me, giving me a light-hearted smile. I felt my heart beat faster. Looking away, I didn't know what to do since we were the only ones sitting on the floor. Not making much eye contact or conversation, I stole glances out from the corner of my eye. Everyone was having a good time, socializing and bonding, and yet I was so nervous that all I managed to do was awkwardly laugh at everything. He soon got up, maybe because I wasn't speaking to him or maybe he just grew tired from sitting on the floor? But I felt somewhat disappointed.

Letting it go, I too stood up and made my way inside to place my phone on charge. Remembering how I left John on reading, I ignored Spots too. I could tell Spots was serious about me and yet my heart refused to go his way. Was I made of stone? I could not accept the sincerity of someone who was trying to win me over. I could only think of myself and how my heart has grown tired. How I'm slowly losing myself, how I see a stranger in the mirror and how I drown in my tears. How life had given me a reason to give up.

Pushing the thought out of my head, I returned to the big group. Everyone seemed happy as if their need for socialization had been filled. Accepting that I won't be speaking much, Zack interrupted my train of thought.

"Have you seen the new Dragon Ball movie?" I looked at him and softly said no. I knew he was a fan of anime, I just never knew he would speak to me. Do you even like DBZ? He asked, hoping for me to say yes.

"No, I don't like it," I replied honestly. He looked surprised and yet he never stopped smiling at me. Was he trying to speak to me? Me, Invisible Melissa? I couldn't help but smile back at him. If these were signs then I wouldn't mind playing along.

Sitting on the floor yet again, Zack didn't hesitate to join. These were definitely signs. Either I was hallucinating or he was actually giving off a certain vibe. Before I could give much thought to it, Shannon spoke.

"Melissa doesn't like Lilith either." As she spoke to Zack he turned to me with a smile. Zack hates her." Shannon looked at me and I looked at Zack. He looked happy as he stuck his hand out for a high five. Feeling something in my stomach drop, I realized he wasn't truly over her the moment I saw him give off a sad smile. Could I blame him? They were dating for years until she decided to cheat on him. I had no place in his life and yet I felt the urge to help him move on.

Rethinking the lift club, I might actually accept it. I didn't understand it but I felt drawn to him. It could be that I would find the missing piece to my puzzle if I get to know him. But, what if it's a mistake? Growing attached to a new friendship only to watch it fall apart. Was I ready to have another knife pierce my heart? Or will he be able to heal the wounds I could never mend?

CHAPTER FOUR

"I'm suffocating inside?"

My head was throbbing. Morning has come and yet everything felt as dark as night. I couldn't get last night out of my head, all the what-ifs playing like a recorder in my mind. I was playing with fire and yet, I didn't mind getting burnt if it meant warming this ice-cold heart. What was I searching for, why was I not content with what I had, how am I still alive when I'm suffocating inside?

Looking at my phone, I saw a delightful message from John. He was furious at the fact that I didn't reply to him yesterday. Understandable, and yet I couldn't care less. Hating myself for feeling this way, I decided enough was enough. It was time to put my heart at ease by returning his. I couldn't be his home when I have yet to find my own.

Reading his message, I felt the pain in his words. Feeling the last breath of air escape my lungs as he clung on even harder, it was time for him to let go. Instead of replying, I put my phone down. I had to focus on Brians's graduation; it was supposed to be a happy day.

I was proud of my brother, despite all the setbacks he had in life, he always pushed above it. He was my role model, someone who I aimed to be. Today was his day, the family got together to celebrate his graduation, his accomplishment.

Eventually, the whole family showed up. Keith, my cousin who was my age, sat down next to me. Keith treated me more as intellectual competition than actual blood. He would say I'm his favorite cousin, but I had a feeling there was more to it than that, almost as though he still held a grudge against me that would never heal. I cannot take back my actions, I cannot swallow my words but I tried to redeem his trust, even though I knew it was merely a dream.

In all honesty, I wasn't very fond of some of the family members from my Dad's side of the family, but I pretended for everyone's sake. Maybe it was wrong of me to feel this way, but they never took an interest in how we felt. It was always my Father. How he felt and what he said. Everyone believed his lies but never confronted us. It was us against him and his family. Maybe one-day things would change but the wind was blowing me in a direction far from them. Whether or not I returned, depended on whether anything changed along the way.

Staring at the clock, hours had passed by. I had to reply. Reading his messages, he explained how I hurt him by not replying to him, that he was concerned, that what I had done wasn't right. Acknowledging my mistake, it was too late to turn around. Replying, I admitted to being in the wrong and also that I no longer wanted a relationship. I felt numb, almost as though I had lost the ability to feel.

This feeling had been coming on for a while. I had given up on love; I had given up on happiness. Smiling every day, nobody ever knew the truth. I couldn't admit I was depressed. I lost myself years ago, I needed someone to guide me back to the light but instead, I walked deeper into the darkness. My home became a living nightmare and prison. The whispering secrets kept within my room haunted me. Nobody ever understood me, nobody ever saw the person hidden behind this mask.

Keith interrupted my train of thought, confiding in him, I told him I left John. He was surprised. He believed we were very happy together. I shrugged.

At one point we were. He helped me through a lot and I appreciate it but I can't do this anymore. That's right; my heart and soul had kicked him out. I was no longer looking for security; I was looking for comfort and growth, something which he could not provide. Taking the scissors, I cut the string. After a long road, I was finally free.

"I understand, if you want to leave then it's okay." He replied, I sadly smiled at him. Brian, James, and Vincent made their way past us. Looking ready to leave before anybody else showed up. I hopped towards them.

"Where are you going?"

"Taking a drive," Brian answered eager to getaway.

"Can we join you guys?" As I looked towards Keith, I saw a change in his facial expression. I wasn't even surprised; they never wanted to be with us. Possibly another family grudge aimed at my mother's family or even my family. Rumors and false accusations never seemed to surprise me.

"I think we're going home now actually," Keith said hesitantly. Watching him indicate to his mother, I chose to ignore it.

"Okay, I'm going then. Bye." I could not change their minds, nor did I have the energy to deal with something so petty.

Checking my phone once again, John explained his confusion and pain. How he thought we would last, how he thought I would always fight. At one point, I thought the same, but he was meant to be nothing more than a friend. It's a shame I realized that too late. Replying, I gave him no closure. I just wanted it all to end.

Drowning in my thoughts, I needed to escape. I felt his grip let go, but I wouldn't be able to cushion his fall. Looking at the night sky, I closed my eyes. When will this darkness ever fade? Drowning in my sorrows, I needed to swim even if it was only for a few hours. Looking at the glass in my hand, I began to hate myself.

Suddenly my mind drifted to the lift club, it was now or never. I no longer had strings attached, I no longer had fears, I could now wander as far as my heart wanted to.

"Vincent. Can I have Shannon's number please?" He looked at me in confusion.

"Why?" I knew he would ask that, guess I have to explain myself.

"Shannon offered me a ride in Zacks lift club but I don't have her number. Could I please get it before my battery dies?"

"Okay, I'll read it out loud for you." I sighed, really now?

"Pleeease, I'll be quick," I begged, he eventually gave in.

Managing to get her number, I wondered if this was a good idea. What if I was rushing into something that wasn't meant to happen? Staring at her number, I hesitantly entered the chat. Sending a message, it showed one tick. Great, another way to eat at my nervousness.

I couldn't help but wonder where I went wrong. Why do I keep running? I had no destination in mind and yet I kept pushing, even when my legs felt as though they were giving in. It was the first night that I no longer carried the burden of guilt. I no longer needed to lie to everyone about my relationship status. No idea as to what relationship status that was, I sighed.

I just tore someone's heart into pieces and I had no remorse. I wondered what Zack was like and how I wanted to help him. I felt myself smile as I realized I finally took the leap I've been waiting for. Maybe it would be a complete fail, maybe it would blossom into a beautiful friendship.

Was I ready? I lost those who meant the world to me. I was never good at keeping friendships going. Maybe I would walk away from him too. I wasn't sure what to do. Doubts played in my mind, getting louder and louder with each thought. I wanted to do this, I was curious as to who Zack was and what made him tick. I was ready to open up to someone but first I needed comfort.

Making our way home, I refused to look at my phone. The atmosphere was dense, you wouldn't think a celebration was held here. I wasn't surprised. My mom's family had no place in this house, or so my father made it out to be. It made no sense, but nobody could fix a tainted heart. My dad strongly believed that my mom's family was the root of the problem.

Whenever there would be a fight, my dad would bring up her family. It was a storm that held no rainbow. We never saw the end of it. It broke us apart. I felt as though I had been placed in the middle. That my Last Name was just a name, that my blood wasn't important, that there would never be a balance in life. I could never look at my dad with the respect he deserved. Some part of me knew I would end up just like him and I was ready to put an end to it before that ever happened. Even if it meant never seeing the break of dawn ever again. I made my way to bed, pushing out everything thought that could disturb the small amount of peace I had.